EMILY and SAM

The Spelling Bee Showdown

A Reading Adventure

Don't miss Emily and Sam's other adventures!

1. The Case of the Missing Turtle
2. The Mad Scientist Next Door

EMILY and SAM

The Spelling Bee Showdown

A Reading Adventure

Book 3

in the **EMILY** and **SAM** Series

by

Dave Cole

Common Deer Press

Published by Common Deer Press Incorporated

Published in 2025 by Common Deer Press
1745 Rockland Avenue
Victoria, British Columbia
V8S 1W6

Library and Archives Canada Cataloguing in Publication

Title: Emily and Sam : the spelling bee showdown :
a reading adventure / by Dave Cole.
Other titles: Spelling bee showdown
Names: Cole, David, 1957- author. | Mitchell, Matty, illustrator.
Description: Series statement: Book 3 in the Emily and Sam series |
Illustrated by Matty Mitchell.
Identifiers: Canadiana (print) 2024040128X |
Canadiana (ebook) 20240412761 | ISBN 9781998484027
(softcover) | ISBN 9781998484034 (EPUB)
Subjects: LCGFT: School fiction. | LCGFT: Novels.
Classification: LCC PZ7.1.C64 Ems 2025 | DDC j813/.6—dc23

Cover Image: Matty Mitchell
Book Design: David Moratto

Printed in Canada
www.CommonDeerPress.com

To Justin, for making me
such a proud father

Mrs. Gunther's Announcements

The Hilbert twins, Emily and Sam, had always been in the same classroom. That was fine with them because they were best friends as well as brother and sister. But that didn't mean they were exactly alike. When it came to school, Emily loved reading and science, while Sam preferred spelling and math. Those differences were very clear when Mrs. Gunther, their teacher, made two big announcements one morning.

"We're going to be starting a literary unit on *Aesop's Fables,*" she told the class.

Sam groaned quietly to himself. It sounded like a lot of reading to him.

Michelle Gabriel's hand shot up in the front row. Sam looked at his sister, who sat two desks away from him. They both rolled their eyes: they knew exactly what Michelle was going to ask.

"What's a fable?" she asked.

"A fable is a special kind of story that teaches a lesson," Mrs. Gunther answered. "The characters are often animals or plants who talk and act like people. These stories have been passed down from generation to generation over thousands of years. We'll be studying fables from Aesop, one of the most famous storytellers of all time. Aesop was a man who lived in Greece more than two thousand years ago, and his fables were collected into a book called *Aesop's Fables.* Now, here's the fun part—at the end of the unit, we'll work in pairs to write our own stories. I'll put all of these into a book called *Gunther's Fables,* and you'll each get a copy."

A few of the students groaned out loud. Sam was one of them. If there was anything he hated more than reading, it was writing.

Unlike her brother, Emily was super excited. She loved to read and write her own stories. Before Mrs. Gunther had even finished talking about the project, Emily was jotting down ideas for stories.

"And now for my second bit of exciting news," Mrs. Gunther said. Everyone sat up straight at their desks, curious about what would come next. "We're going to have an all-school spelling bee."

Now it was Emily's turn to groan. Emily was a pretty good speller, but it was still one of her least favorite subjects. Two desks over, Sam was grinning ear to ear. He loved spelling. Sam liked learning new tricks to spell words, like the one his dad had taught him about knowing the difference between *principle* (a belief) and *principal* (the head of the school). He remembered that "the principal is his pal," so that was the one that ended in *p-a-l*.

"Our class competition will be a week from Friday," continued Mrs. Gunther. "The winner will go on to face the winners from the other classes the following week. There are sample spelling lists on my desk. Please take one home to study."

Emily trudged up to her teacher's desk and picked up a thick pile of papers stapled together. She shook her head as she paged through the packet. There were hundreds of words. Maybe even thousands! There was no way she was going to learn how to spell all of these words in the next week.

At lunch, Emily sat with her brother Sam in the cafeteria. Both were quiet. Emily just pushed her food around the tray instead of eating. All she could think about was that endless list of spelling words. Sam was eating—nothing could ever bother him enough to spoil his appetite—but his mind was on the fable he didn't want to write.

"I can't believe we have to write some stupid story," Sam complained while he snatched a couple of carrot sticks from his sister's tray.

"Yeah? Well, that sure beats having to memorize a bunch of silly words," Emily replied. She moved the rest of her carrots to Sam's tray.

"Spelling is fun. I bet I'll win our class competition," Sam bragged.

"I read more than you," said Emily.

"So?"

"So that means I probably know a lot more words than you."

"Maybe, but can you spell them?" Sam teased.

"I could beat you in the spelling bee if I tried," Emily said.

"Not in a million years," Sam snorted.

"I bet I could."

Sam grinned. This competition would sure be interesting. "Okay," he said, "what do you want to bet?"

Emily thought for a long moment while Sam looked on in anticipation.

"Earth to Emily," he said, tapping his finger on his wrist. "You going to bet today or what?"

Emily didn't really want to bet against her brother because she wasn't sure she could actually beat him. The problem was, she was the one who had suggested the bet. There was no way she could get out of it now. But maybe she could get Sam to back out if she bet something he really didn't want to lose. Finally, she came up with just the right thing!

Emily smiled sweetly at her brother. "The loser has to write our story for *Gunther's Fables*."

Sam's face went pale. He hated to write, especially if his story was going to be read by all his classmates.

"Well?" Emily prompted.

"Fine," Sam snapped. "You're on."

Sam extended his hand across the table and Emily shook it, but both of them looked worried. Had they just made a big mistake?

New Classmates

Mrs. Gunther had more surprises in store the next morning. When she walked into the classroom, she was followed by another woman and two boys Sam and Emily hadn't seen before.

"Can I get everyone's attention?" Mrs. Gunther called out in a loud voice. The class settled into their seats, interested in learning about their visitors.

Mrs. Gunther put her hand lightly on the shoulder of the shorter of the two boys. He had slanted eyes and a slightly flattened nose in the center of his round face. His hair was very blond, almost white, and was trimmed into a crew cut.

"This is Drew Taylor," Mrs. Gunther said.

"He'll be joining our class several times a week." Mrs. Gunther then nodded at the woman. "And this is his aide, Ms. Santos, who'll be helping Drew while he is in our class. Please make them both feel welcome."

Sam and Emily politely clapped along with the rest of the class. Drew gave a shy smile. He quietly mumbled "hello" while barely lifting his gaze from the floor.

"What's your favorite thing to do, Drew?" asked Mrs. Gunther.

Drew looked up slightly and quietly said, "Movies."

"You like watching movies?" the teacher asked, encouraging the boy. Drew nodded. "What kind of movies do you like to watch?"

"*Little Mermaid* and *Mulan* and *Lion King*," Drew said, a smile coming to his lips.

Drew's speech was a little difficult to understand and there were a few laughs from the class. Sam noticed how the boy's smile faded. Mrs. Gunther looked out across the room and the laughter stopped under her stern stare.

"Those are some of my favorites too," she said to Drew. "It's good to have you with us."

"Thanks," Drew mumbled, his gaze back on the floor.

Ms. Santos led the boy to a seat near the back of the room.

Turning to the other boy, Mrs. Gunther continued, "And this young man is Nicholas Bryson. He and his family just moved here from Washington, DC. Can you tell us a little about yourself, Nicholas?"

"You can call me Nick," the new boy said confidently. He was tall and had thick brown hair that he flipped out of his eyes as he spoke. "My dad works for the CIA. I guess you could say he's kind of a super spy, like James Bond. I love to play soccer. I was the leading scorer on my team. My sister is a gymnast. Her coach says she'll probably make the Olympic team. My mom used to work in the White House."

There was more, but Sam had already heard enough. His jaw had dropped as soon as Nick began to speak.

At lunch, all the boys in the class wanted to sit with Nick. They crowded around the new kid and flooded him with questions.

"Can you tell us about any of your dad's cases?"

"I'm sorry, but that information is classified." Laughs from everyone at the table.

"Have you ever met the president?"

"Sure, who hasn't?" This was met with oohs and aahs.

"Can your sister do a double backflip?"

"Of course, only she does hers with a full twist." More oohs and aahs.

"Will you play on my soccer team?"

"Maybe, but I'll have to check out how good you guys are first."

Like all the other boys, Sam was in awe of the new kid. He couldn't wait for lunch to end so they could get out to recess. It was Sam's turn to be one of the captains when they chose teams for soccer. He was already planning on selecting Nick with his first pick!

When the recess bell finally rang, the kids hurried out to the playground. As he went through the door, Sam looked back and noticed there was only one boy left behind. In the back of the cafeteria, Drew ate his lunch alone.

Emily's Spelling Problem

"*I* before *e*, except after *c*, or when it sounds like *a* in *neighbor* and *weigh*," Emily said.

She was sitting alone in her bedroom, studying a list of spelling rules. She hoped the rules would help her prepare for the spelling bee but she was only getting more and more frustrated.

"Except that rule doesn't work for words like *weird* or *science* or *forfeit*," she sighed. "What good is a rule when it doesn't work all the time?"

She threw her list of spelling rules onto her bed. "This is hopeless!" she cried out.

"Are you talking to me?" her dad asked as he poked his head into the bedroom, a steaming cup of coffee in one hand.

"No, it's these stupid spelling rules," she said. "Why can't I learn to spell like Sam?"

Her dad looked at her over his cup of coffee.

"Who says you can't?" he asked.

"It doesn't make any sense," she said. "I read lots more books than Sam, so I should be able to spell better than him."

"Spelling is harder than reading," her dad explained. He sat down on the bed next to Emily. "When you are reading and see a new word, you can usually figure out how to say the word by looking at the letters. It's much harder to hear a word and then figure out how to spell it. There are only twenty-six letters in the alphabet, but those letters make forty-five sounds. And there are more than 250 ways to spell those sounds."

Emily groaned. "If that's supposed to make me feel better, it's not working," she said. "I might as well give up."

"That doesn't sound like my Emily," her dad said. He placed a hand on her shoulder and gave her a comforting pat. "Can I offer you two pieces of advice?"

"I guess."

"First of all, forget about all the spelling rules," he said. "They can help a little, but there

are so many exceptions that they might actually make things harder for you. Just trust yourself. The way you think a word is spelled is probably the way it *is* spelled. If not, you miss the word. It's not a big deal."

"It is when missing a word means your brother beats you," Emily snipped.

"So that's what this is about," her dad said. "You and your brother are in a spelling bee at school?"

"Yeah. The first one is just our class, but the winner goes on to the school-wide spelling bee."

"If it's you against your brother, maybe I should stay out of it," he said.

"No!" Emily protested. "You help him with spelling all the time. I'm just trying to catch up."

Her dad took a drink of coffee and put on his serious face. "Okay, I'll help . . . under one condition. Win or lose, he's still your brother and that's more important than any spelling bee. Agreed?"

Emily thought about that for a moment, then nodded her head in agreement.

Her dad picked up the list of spelling rules and looked at them for a minute. "Your brother likes all the spelling rules," her dad said, "but if I were you, I would start by reading through the list of words your teacher gave you. You probably already know how to spell most of them, so just circle the ones you don't know. Those are the ones you have to study."

"That's still a lot of work," Emily said.

"Most things in life that you really want take some work," he said.

"Okay, mark off the words I don't know how to spell," Emily said. "You said you had two pieces of advice. What's the second one?"

"Right. Well, do you remember how frustrated you were when Sam learned how to ride his bike before you did?" her dad asked.

"Do I? It was horrible. He was riding up and down the street while I was going around in circles on the driveway with my training wheels still on."

"Can you ride your bike now?"

"Of course," Emily said. "I'm even faster than Sam."

"How'd you get from training wheels to speeding down the street?"

"I just kept practicing," she said.

Her dad nodded.

"So, what you're saying is learning to spell is like learning to ride a bike?" Emily asked.

"Except with a lot fewer skinned knees and elbows," he answered with a smile.

"Okay, I guess it's time I learn to ride," she said. "Maybe my studying would go better with a snack. I'll be in the kitchen if you need me."

She was almost out of her room when her dad called her back. He held up her list of spelling words. "I think you forgot your training wheels," he said.

The Ant and the Grasshopper

Ever since Nick joined Mrs. Gunther's class, Sam had been trying to spend as much time with the new kid as he could. Instead of walking to school with Emily and Mateo, their next-door neighbor, Sam went three blocks out of his way to Nick's house.

"Hey Nick!" Sam said as soon as Nick stepped out onto his front porch.

"Hi Sam. Hey Josh," Nick called out.

Sam looked around and saw Josh Choi running toward them. Sam was annoyed. Josh was okay, but Sam thought he was trying too hard to get Nick to like him.

"Did you watch the new episode of *Zombies on the Moon* last night?" Josh asked while bending over to try to catch his breath.

"Yeah, it was pretty cool," Nick said. "You watch it, Sam?"

"No," Sam replied. "I was finishing my math homework."

"Math homework?" Nick snorted. "Those problems were so easy I didn't bother doing the homework. Besides, I didn't want to miss the show."

"But we have to turn our homework in," Sam pointed out.

"At my last school, as long as you knew how to solve the problems, you didn't have to turn in homework."

"That makes sense," Josh agreed.

"Well, Mrs. Gunther makes us turn it in," Sam said.

"Really?" Nick asked. "Can I just copy yours when we get to school?"

"Yeah, I guess that would be okay," Sam said.

"Then we'd better get moving," Nick said, turning and walking away quickly, with Josh right on his heels. Sam followed the two boys, a troubled expression on his face.

When they got to school, Nick quickly copied Sam's homework and slipped the answers into his notebook, finishing just as Mrs. Gunther walked into the room.

To Sam's dismay, the teacher already had the large book of fables in her hand.

After collecting the homework, Mrs. Gunther opened the storybook. "Okay class, today we're going to talk about another of Aesop's fables," she announced. "This one is called *The Ant and the Grasshopper.*"

The class settled in as Mrs. Gunther told the tale.

"Once there was a grasshopper and an ant that lived in the countryside. During the summer, the grasshopper played all day. There was plenty of sunshine and lots of grass to eat, so he had a merry time dancing in the fields. The ant, on the other hand, worked hard all summer. He gathered sweet plants, seeds, grass, and leaves and stored them in his ant hill.

'Why do you spend all your time working when you could be playing?' the grasshopper asked.

'I want to be prepared when the winter comes and there is no food,' the ant answered.

'But there is food all around us,' the grasshopper said, dancing around the ant merrily.

'Winter will be here before you know it,' the ant answered, tugging a large leaf toward the entrance to his ant hill.

'You work too hard,' the grasshopper said.
'You play too much,' the ant replied.

As the days went by, the weather began to cool. Leaves turned red and yellow and fell from the trees.

The grasshopper made piles of leaves and jumped into them, laughing and playing.

Meanwhile, the ant worked even harder, collecting seeds and grass, and storing them away in his ant hill.

Finally, the last leaves fell, and the trees were bare. The grass turned brown and died. The cold winds came and blew across the fields. Snowflakes began to fall to the ground, just a few at first but then more and more until the fields were covered in white.

In his ant hill home, the ant snuggled under a warm leaf and nibbled on a tasty seed.

Outside, the wind howled. It was so loud the ant could barely hear the sound of the grasshopper calling for help.

'What is it?' the ant asked as he popped his head up from the top of the ant hill.

'It's cold and I'm hungry,' the grasshopper wailed.

'Didn't you store up any food for the winter?' the ant asked.

'I didn't have time,' the grasshopper said.

'It's because you spent all your time playing and dancing,' the ant reminded the grasshopper.

'Can you spare some of your food for me?' the grasshopper asked.

'No,' said the ant. 'It's not my fault you didn't prepare for winter.'

Without another word, the ant dropped back down into his warm, cozy home full of food, leaving the grasshopper wailing in the winter storm."

Mrs. Gunther closed her book and looked at the class. "Well, what do you think?"

"I think the ant was mean," said Susan O'Reilly. "He had plenty of food but wouldn't share it."

"In some versions of the fable, the ant shares his food with the grasshopper," Mrs. Gunther said.

"I wouldn't have shared it," said Josh.

"Why not?" Mrs. Gunther asked.

"It was the grasshopper's fault he didn't store up any food for the winter," Josh explained. "If he had saved up like the ant did, he would have had food to eat."

"If I were the grasshopper, I'd just take the food," Nick said. "I mean, a grasshopper is a lot bigger than an ant. I'd just destroy the ant hill and eat everything."

"That's certainly a different way to look at it," said Mrs. Gunther. "What do you think about Nick's approach, Sam?"

Sam looked over at Nick. "Nick's right that the grasshopper could just take the food. But just because you can do something doesn't mean that's what you should do."

The class continued to talk about the fable, but for the rest of the day Sam couldn't get his mind off what Nick had said.

That night, Sam had trouble falling asleep. When he finally drifted off, he dreamt about an ant and a grasshopper. In his dream, the ant worked hard on his math homework while the grasshopper watched *Zombies on the Moon*. When it was time to turn in their homework, the grasshopper didn't have his done. He begged the ant to let him copy his homework. The ant didn't want to lose the grasshopper's friendship, so he let him copy his work. "What a sucker!" the grasshopper said as he hopped merrily away.

Sam didn't remember his dream the next morning, but he decided he wouldn't be sharing his homework with Nick ever again.

The Tortoise and the Hare

The morning after Sam's bad dream, Emily walked into the kitchen without a word. She sat down across from her brother, dropping her list of spelling words on the table next to her. She grabbed a piece of toast and a glass of orange juice and ate while spelling words to herself.

"You're quiet this morning," her mom said.

Emily just nodded without looking up from her word list.

"How's the spelling coming?" asked Sam.

"Fine," Emily said.

"Getting a little worried?" he asked. "The spelling bee is next week."

"Don't you think I know that?" Emily snipped.

"Whoa! Someone is sure *t-o-u-c-h-y* this morning," Sam teased.

Emily ignored him and turned her attention back to the list.

"Maybe you should just give up," Sam said.

"And maybe you should be studying instead of bothering me," Emily shot back.

"I've got plenty of time," he replied confidently.

"Sounds like you didn't get the moral of the tortoise and the hare fable," Emily said.

Sam looked confused. "The what?"

"The fable we were supposed to read last night." Emily said. "You know, the one you obviously didn't read."

"I was going to get to it," Sam said.

"That's what the rabbit said," Emily replied, smirking.

"Well, what's the fable?" he asked.

"I'm surprised you don't already know this one, Sam," his mom answered. "It's one of the most famous stories out there. There was once a race between a tortoise and a hare. The hare started off quickly and was soon far ahead of the tortoise. He was so far ahead that he decided to take a nap. In the meantime, the tortoise kept plodding along, step by step, never stopping. He passed the hare who was still napping. It wasn't until the tortoise was close to the finish line that the hare finally woke up. Seeing that the tortoise was in front of him, the hare ran as fast as he could, but it was too late. The tortoise won. The moral of the story is that slow and steady wins the race."

"Slow and steady wins the race," Sam repeated. "What's that got to do with spelling?"

"Emily is studying her spelling every day. It sounds like your plan is to wait until the last minute and then try to catch up," his mom said.

Sam laughed. "There's no way that Emily the tortoise is ever going to catch up to Sam the hare. Face it, Emily. You can't beat me. Now, hurry up and get your stuff. We need to get to school."

"Aren't you going to walk with your best friend Nick?" Emily said.

"Nah, I thought I'd walk with you and Mateo today," Sam said.

"You don't need to do us any favors," Emily snapped as she got up from the table. She gathered her papers and stomped out of the kitchen.

"What was that all about?" Sam's mom asked.

"Nothing," Sam answered.

"Nothing?" his mom said with a raised eyebrow. "It sure looked like something to me."

"She's just mad because I'm going to beat her in the class spelling bee."

"Maybe instead of teasing her, you could help her with her studying," his mom pointed out.

"But I want to beat her," Sam said.

“Winning isn’t everything,” his mom said.

“Maybe not, but it’s better than losing.”

“Not if winning a small thing costs you a big thing,” she said.

Sam was still thinking about what his mom had said as he walked to school by himself.

A Wolf in Sheep's Clothing

That weekend, the twins barely spoke to each other. Emily was focused on practicing her spelling and Sam couldn't seem to stop thinking about the fables.

Back in school on Monday, Mrs. Gunther again pulled out her large book of fables. Emily sat upright in her seat, paying close attention and glad to get the spelling bee off her mind for a while. Even Sam looked like he was interested.

"Once there was a wolf who lived in the woods near a field of sheep," Mrs. Gunther began. "He was very hungry and wanted to eat one of the sheep, but every time he got close, the shepherd and his dogs would chase the wolf away.

As the wolf hungrily roamed the woods around the sheep pasture, he found the skin of a sheep that had been thrown aside. He wrapped the fleece carefully around him so none of his fur was showing. Now he looked just like one of the sheep! He was able to walk among the sheep without the shepherd or his dogs chasing him away. At night, he would lure one of the lambs into the woods and have him for dinner. This went on for many days without the wolf being caught.

But one day, the shepherd decided he would cook a lamb for his own dinner. He chose the fattest sheep he could find and killed him on the spot. What a surprise he got when he found out he had just killed the wolf!"

Mrs. Gunther looked out across the classroom. "What do you think about that story?"

"It was pretty short," Yasmin Khalid said.

"Most fables are," said Mrs. Gunther, nodding. "But that doesn't mean they can't provide a good lesson for us. In fact, this fable has two morals. Who can give me one of them?"

In the back of the room, Drew raised his hand. Mrs. Gunther looked surprised—it was the first time Drew had raised his hand in class. "Yes, Drew?"

"Three pigs," he said. Nick and some of the other boys laughed. Sam looked over at Nick and frowned.

"Three pigs?" Mrs. Gunther repeated as she walked closer to Drew so she could hear his quiet voice.

"Little pigs," Drew said.

"Are you talking about the story of the three little pigs and the wolf?" Mrs. Gunther asked.

Drew nodded excitedly. "Huff and puff and blow your house down!"

Now more of the class was laughing. A stern look from their teacher silenced everyone.

"Some of you laughed, but Drew is right. The first moral of the story is beware of a wolf. Especially if the wolf is wearing sheep's clothing. Good job, Drew!"

She bumped fists with Drew, earning a big grin from the boy.

Mrs. Gunther walked back to the front of the room. "Beware of a wolf in sheep's clothing," she repeated. "That's a common phrase. But what do you think it means?"

Emily raised her hand. When the teacher called on her, she said "I think it means that sometimes people are not always who we think they are."

"That's right," Mrs. Gunther agreed. "A person sometimes might appear to be friendly or harmless, when underneath their disguise they are really something else. Anyone have a guess about the second lesson?"

She looked around the classroom. When no one raised their hand, she asked, "What happened to the wolf?"

"It got eaten," Josh called out.

"So the lesson is?" Mrs. Gunther prompted.

"Don't get eaten?" Josh answered. The class erupted in laughter. Even Mrs. Gunther joined in.

"Close," she said. "The lesson is if you pretend to be something you're not, you might get caught. While you probably won't get eaten like the wolf in our story, you may not like what happens to you."

At lunch, Sam sat down across from Emily. She looked up in surprise.

"Why aren't you sitting with Nick?" she asked.

"His table was full," Sam answered.

"*His* table? Since when do people get their own table in the cafeteria?" Emily smirked.

Sam didn't answer. He took a big bite of his turkey sandwich, a dab of mustard dropping onto his shirt. He tried to wipe it off with a napkin, but only managed to make the yellow spot even bigger. Emily tried to hide her smile but wasn't successful. Sam saw the grin and got mad. He grabbed his lunch and moved to the only table with an available seat. He found himself at a table with Drew, the other new kid.

"Hello, Sam," Drew said.

"Hey," Sam said.

"*S-a-m* spells *Sam*."

"Yeah."

"Spot," Drew said, pointing at Sam's shirt.

"Don't you think I know that?" Sam snapped back.

"Me too," Drew said, standing up to show Sam a splotch of jelly on his jeans.

Sam nodded.

"You look sad," Drew said. He handed Sam one of his chocolate chip cookies.

Sam gave the boy a half-smile. Chocolate chip cookies couldn't fix everything, but they sure helped.

DRE

The Wolf Gets Caught

Two days later, Emily and Sam were sitting at the breakfast table with their parents.

"Is there a race to see who can finish their breakfast first?" Sam's dad asked.

Sam looked up from the bowl of cereal he was scarfing down like his life depended on it.

"No, I just want to get to school early today," Sam said. "Nick's dad is going to drop him off."

"Is he the one who works for the CIA?" his mom asked.

"Yeah, Nick says he's one of their top spies," said Sam. "I bet he's been all over the world. Josh Choi says he speaks like ten languages and has all kinds of cool spy gadgets. I hope he'll have some of them with him in the car."

"Well, Nick's dad certainly sounds interesting," his mom replied. "Does anyone want any more cereal?"

"I'm too excited to eat," Sam replied, but then held out his empty bowl. "Okay, maybe just one more bowlful."

His mom laughed and poured cereal into his bowl and handed him the milk. "Your stomach is like a bottomless pit."

"How about you, Emily?" her dad asked.

"Cereal? No, thanks," Emily replied.

"I was talking about Nick's dad," her dad said. "Are you excited to see a real spy?"

"I guess," Emily said. "It's just that . . ."

"It's just that what?" Sam asked.

"Well, I think sometimes Nick stretches the truth," Emily answered.

"Are you calling him a liar?" Sam asked loudly.

"I didn't say that," Emily replied sharply. "I just said he exaggerates once in a while."

"Well, you'll see when we meet him," Sam said.

The twins walked to school together, but neither one said a word. Emily thought it was better than fighting, at least. It seemed that since they had bet on the spelling bee, they had done nothing but argue.

When they arrived in front of the school, there was a crowd of kids waiting eagerly. Emily shook her head and headed for the entrance.

"Aren't you going to stay to meet Nick's dad?" Sam asked.

"No, I'm going to study for the spelling bee," she answered. "I could use some help if you've got a few minutes."

"No way!" Sam said. "I'm not missing out on this."

Their neighbor Mateo overheard the conversation as he came walking up. "I'll give you a hand," he told Emily.

Emily and Mateo walked into the school, leaving the crowd of boys behind.

There was a stirring in the crowd as a brown car turned into the drop-off area.

"It's him!" called someone from the front. The boys pushed forward. The car pulled to a stop and Nick emerged with a big grin on his face.

"My fans are here," he quipped. The boys stared past him into the car.

The driver's side door opened and Nick's dad stepped out of the car. Mr. Bryson was not what Sam had imagined. He was short and a little plump, with black glasses perched on the end of his nose. He was mostly bald, with just patches of thin brown hair on the sides of his head. He was hardly the picture of a super spy.

"Do you really work for the CIA?" Josh asked.

Mr. Bryson smiled. "I do. In fact, I personally saved all of the spies who work for the CIA."

The crowd oohed and aahed. Sam edged forward for a better view. This was getting good!

"You see, I work in accounting," Mr. Bryson went on.

Accounting? Sam frowned. Nick's dad wasn't a super spy?

"I make sure our spies are paying the right amount for their taxes and benefits," Nick's dad continued. "So, in a way, I guess you can say I saved all of them . . . some money." He gave a wink before getting back in his car and driving away.

The angry crowd of boys surrounded Nick.

"Your dad's not a spy," Josh accused Nick.

"Do you think he could tell you about his real job?" Nick protested.

"Yeah, we did," Arvind Singh replied.

"Well, you were the ones who said you wanted to meet him so bad," Nick pointed out.

CIA

"But why would he make stuff up?" Tomas Fernandez asked.

"That's what spies do," Nick said. "That accounting thing is just his cover story."

"Yeah, right," Josh snorted. "Come on, guys, let's go to the playground. My dad should be landing in his spaceship soon."

Sam watched as the boys walked away in a chorus of laughter, leaving Nick fuming behind them. Sam tried to think of what to say to him, but he was still confused by what he had just seen. Nick had told everyone his dad was a spy at the CIA, but it turns out that was all made up. Was Emily right about Nick?

Drew took the wrong time to arrive at school. As Nick turned to stomp away, he bumped into the smaller boy. Furious, Nick shoved Drew, knocking him to the ground. Drew looked up at Nick in confusion.

"Watch where you're going!" Nick yelled as he clomped off.

Sam stared after him, then bent to help Drew to his feet.

"He pushed me," Drew said.

"Yeah, he did," Sam replied.

"Why?"

"He was mad that people found out he wasn't what he was pretending to be," Sam explained.

Sam could see that Drew didn't understand what he was saying, so he tried to explain another way.

"Do you remember that story about the wolf?" Sam asked.

"Huff and puff and blow your house down," Drew said.

"Yeah," said Sam. "Well, it turns out Nick is the wolf."

The Fox and the Grapes

"Like most of the fables we've been reading, this one is pretty short," Mrs. Gunther began as the class settled into their seats to start the day. "It's called *The Fox and the Grapes.*"

"How many of these stories do we have to hear?" Sam whispered to Tomas.

Emily, two rows over from Sam, also heard what he said and grinned at her brother. Sam stuck his tongue out at her, hiding it behind his hand so the teacher wouldn't see.

Mrs. Gunther heard the whisper and saw Sam stick his tongue out but chose to ignore both. Instead, she opened the book of fables and began to read.

"One summer day a fox was walking along when he saw a bunch of juicy grapes hanging on a vine.

'Those grapes sure look good,' said the fox, 'just perfect for a hot summer day.'

He stretched his front legs above his head, but the grapes were out of his reach. He tried jumping, but couldn't jump high enough to get to the grapes. Even when he took a long run and leap, he still couldn't reach the grapes. He tried again and again, sweating in the hot summer sun, until he finally gave up.

As he walked away, he said 'I didn't want those grapes anyway. They were probably sour.' And so, he trotted off slowly with his tail between his legs."

Mrs. Gunther closed the book and looked out at the class.

"That's it?" asked Michelle.

"That's it," her teacher replied.

"Why is it so short?" Michelle pressed.

"It's important to remember that many of these stories were passed down from person to person over time," Mrs. Gunther explained. "They weren't written into books until much later. That meant the stories had to be kept short so that people could remember them. There's not much to this story, but it still has a valuable lesson. Does anyone know what it is?"

No one answered, so Mrs. Gunther looked directly at Sam. "Sam? What do you think?"

"Um, don't try to get something you really don't want?" Sam guessed.

"Not quite," Mrs. Gunther said. "But hold on to that thought because I want to come back to it."

Emily raised her hand and the teacher pointed at her. "What do you think, Emily?"

"I think it means that when we can't get something we want, we tell ourselves it wasn't any good anyway," Emily said.

"That's exactly right," Mrs. Gunther praised. "You've probably heard the common saying 'sour grapes.' If someone wanted to be the star of a play and only got a small part, they might say something bad about the play. We might say that's sour grapes. Good job, Emily."

"Lucky guess," Sam snorted.

"Now that sounds like sour grapes," Emily teased. Sam stuck his tongue out at her again, not bothering to hide it this time.

"If you're done airing out your tongue, Sam, let's get back to your thought on the fable," Mrs. Gunther said. Sam turned beet red. "Do you remember what you said?"

"Don't try to get something you don't want?" Sam said.

"Kind of," Mrs. Gunther smiled. "Let me read you a fable Aesop used to tell about that."

"Are you kidding me?" Sam looked at his teacher in amazement. "How many fables did this guy come up with?"

"Somewhere around 750," Mrs. Gunther replied. She thumbed through the book and found the fable. "This is another short one. It's called *The Dog and His Reflection*. One day a dog was walking home with a big bone the butcher had given him. As he crossed a narrow footbridge, he happened to look down into the calm water and saw his reflection. But the dog thought he was seeing another dog with an even tastier bone. He dropped his bone and leaped at the other dog, hoping to steal his bone. Instead, he made a big splash and had to swim to shore. He was cold, wet, and no longer had a bone."

Mrs. Gunther looked at Sam. "Can you guess the lesson in this fable, Sam?"

"Don't try to get something you don't want?" Sam said.

"Close," Mrs. Gunther said. "How about don't try to get something you don't really need?"

"Yeah, I guess that makes even more sense," Sam said.

"Another way of putting it is to be happy with what you have," Mrs. Gunther said.

Sam looked over at his sister. Even though he was sure he was going to win the spelling bee, he took out his notebook and jotted down a few thoughts about what his teacher had said just in case.

The Lion and the Mouse

On Thursday, Sam walked into the cafeteria at lunchtime. He looked around the tables but didn't see any empty spots except for at Drew's table at the back. Drew grinned when he saw Sam coming toward him.

"Hey Sam!" Drew yelled out excitedly. "*S-a-m.*"

The loud voice drew attention from some of the other tables. Nick, who had convinced a few of the boys that his dad really *was* a super spy after all, looked over from his table.

"Hey, shut up! We're trying to eat!" Nick called over to Drew. The other boys at the table broke into laughter.

In an instant, Drew's face changed from a broad smile to a frown. He slumped in his chair and looked down at the table.

Sam looked over at the other table and shook his head in disgust. Nick just grinned back at him.

"Just ignore those guys," Sam said as he sat down. There was no response from Drew, who only stared at the table.

Sam reached into his lunch box and pulled out a sugar cookie. "It's not chocolate chip, but will this help?"

Drew looked up and took the cookie from Sam.

"Thanks," Drew mumbled quietly.

The two boys ate in silence. They had almost finished when Nick, Josh, and Arvind came over to their table.

"We're going out to play soccer, Sam," Nick said. "Want to come with us?"

"Can Drew play too?" Sam asked. Drew looked up hopefully.

"Yeah, right," Nick snorted. Josh and Arvind laughed.

"Then I guess I'll hang with him until he finishes his lunch," Sam said.

"Whatever," Nick said. "You can hang with this loser as long as you want."

"He's not a loser," Sam said firmly as he rose from his seat.

"I say he is," Nick said, taking a step toward Sam.

"Well, I think the real loser is someone who picks on people different from them," Sam said.

Nick inched forward, but Sam stood his ground, looking Nick steadily in the eyes.

"Ah, you're not worth it," Nick finally said. "Come on, guys."

Nick turned and walked away, with Josh and Arvind trailing behind him.

Sam looked over at Drew. Sam could see that he was close to tears.

"Sorry, Drew, I'm all out of cookies," Sam said hopelessly, not sure how to make the boy feel better. "I wish there was something I could do."

"You sat with me," Drew said.

"It's no big deal," Sam said, feeling a little embarrassed.

"You're my friend," Drew said. "*F-r-e-n-d.*"

"That's pretty close," Sam said, "but you forgot the *i.*"

Drew looked confused.

"But you know what?" Sam said. "Your spelling makes a lot more sense. *F-r-e-n-d* it is."

Drew nodded and grinned at Sam. "*F-r-e-n-d,*" he said.

Sam sat with Drew while he finished his lunch and then they went to play outside.

Back in class after recess, Mrs. Gunther said something that was music to Sam's ears.

"This is the last story we're going to talk about in our fable unit," she began.

"Yes!" Sam punched his fist in the air. He had heard enough fables.

"This one is called *The Lion and the Mouse,*" Mrs. Gunther said. "One day a lion was sleeping in the forest when a mouse ran across his nose, waking him up. The lion immediately clamped a huge paw on top of the mouse.

Trapped within the lion's claws, the mouse looked up in fright.

'If you free me, I promise I'll repay you some day,' the little mouse said.

'What could you ever do to repay me?' the lion laughed. But he was in a good mood after his nap, so he let the mouse go.

Several days later, the lion was walking through the forest when he got caught in a hunter's net. He clawed and bit at the net, but no matter how hard he tried, he could not free himself. He roared angrily in frustration. The mouse heard the roars and found the lion struggling in the net. The mouse used his sharp little teeth to gnaw on the thick rope until it finally parted and the lion was free.

'You laughed when I said I would repay you,' the mouse pointed out, 'but now you see that even a small mouse can help a mighty lion.'

The lion thanked the mouse and promised

to never doubt the strength of a small creature ever again."

Mrs. Gunther looked over at Nick, who was whispering something to Josh. "What do you think of the story, Nick?" she asked.

Nick's face turned red as he stammered out an answer. "Um, it was good," he said.

"And what do you think the lesson is?" she asked.

"I'll have to think about that a little bit," he said.

"I've got plenty of time," Mrs. Gunther said, smiling at the boy's discomfort.

Nick's face got even redder.

"Is it possible you weren't listening?" Mrs. Gunther asked him.

Nick nodded.

"Anyone else have an idea of what lesson Aesop was trying to teach with this story?" the teacher asked the class.

Michelle raised her hand. "I think it means we shouldn't underestimate someone just because they seem weaker than you."

Mrs. Gunther smiled. "That's right, Michelle. We all have our own strengths, even if others can't see them. We need to treat everyone with respect, but not just when there is something

in it for us. We should do it because it's the right thing to do."

She paused to let those words sink in.

"Okay, we're done with the fables," Mrs. Gunther said. "But remember, the fun part is still coming up. We're going to pair up and write our own stories for *Gunther's Fables,*" she said. "We'll start on that next week. For now, let's concentrate on the class spelling bee tomorrow. I'll give everyone the rest of the afternoon to study the word list."

A feeling of dread fell on Emily. The spelling bee was tomorrow, and she still had so many words to learn. It looked like Sam was going to win their bet. But then she wondered if Sam was underestimating her abilities. Even more importantly, what if she was underestimating herself?

The Spelling Bee

On Friday morning, Sam and Emily walked to school together, but neither had much to say. Emily had studied spelling words until long past her bedtime, and then woke early to look over the words once more. Even Sam had spent hours reviewing the long list of words, confident but not wanting to take any chances.

They were at the front door of the school when Sam tugged Emily's arm to pull her to one side.

"What is it?" she asked.

"Um, I just wanted to say good luck in the spelling bee today," he said.

IMPORTANT
SMART
ANIMAL
HARE
APPEAR
CRAYON
RECEIPT
TORTOISE
BEIGE
ORANGE
INTENTIONAL
PRINCIPLE
PRINCIPAL
FRIEND
DISAPPEAR
BANANA
STORY
WHETHER
DESSERT

She studied his face to see if he was teasing her. Seeing that he was serious, she replied, "Thanks. You too."

"I know you worked really hard to prepare for this," he continued. "I just want you to know that I'm going to try to beat you, but if I don't win, I hope you do."

"Oh, I'm planning on winning," she said with a grin. "But I guess if I don't, I hope it's you."

"Thanks," he said.

"Or maybe Mateo," Emily teased. "Or Michelle, or Josh, or really anyone else."

Sam lightly punched her arm. "So that's the way you're going to be, huh?"

The twins were laughing as they entered the school.

The spelling bee was held first thing in the morning. Mrs. Gunther explained the rules. "You'll line up in alphabetical order by last name. I'll say the word. You can ask me to pronounce it again. You can ask me for the definition of the word or ask me to use the word in a sentence. Then you try to spell the word. If you get it correct, you are through to the next round. If you miss it, you're out of the competition. Does anyone have any questions?"

No one did, and the competition began. Nick was the first to go.

"Your word is *disappear,*" Mrs. Gunther said.

"*Disappear,*" Nick said. "*D-i-s-a-p-e-a-r. Disappear.*"

"I'm sorry, but that's incorrect," Mrs. Gunther said. "The correct spelling is *d-i-s-a-p-p-e-a-r.*"

"That's what I said," Nick protested.

"You only said one *p,*" Mrs. Gunther said.

"I said two," Nick argued. "You must not have heard the second one."

Mrs. Gunther looked over at Drew's aide, Ms. Santos, who shook her head.

"I'm sorry, Nick, but Ms. Santos agrees that you misspelled the word," Mrs. Gunther said. "Please take your seat."

Nick grumbled all the way back to his chair. Sam hid a grin behind his hand.

When it was Emily's turn, she could feel butterflies in her stomach. She was certain she was going to go out in the first round. Luckily, she got an easy word.

"*Banana,*" Mrs. Gunther said.

Emily carefully spelled it out, "*Banana. B-a-n-a-n-a. Banana.*"

"That's correct," Mrs. Gunther said.

Emily let out a sigh of relief.

Sam was next and got the word *important.* Without any hesitation, he quickly spelled it correctly. Drew clapped loudly when Mrs. Gunther said he was right. Drew wasn't part of the spelling bee, but he was watching from his seat at the back of the room.

Mateo went out on the word *beige.* Emily was glad she didn't get that word because she would have spelled it the same way Mateo had and would have been out.

There were twenty-two kids in their classroom, and eleven of them were out at the end of the first round.

At the end of the second round, they were down to seven spellers. By the end of the third round, only Emily, Sam, Michelle, and Josh were left in the competition.

"Well done to our final four spellers," Mrs. Gunther said. "Let's take a ten-minute break and then we'll move on to the next round."

"You're doing great so far," Sam told Emily.

"I'm so nervous with every word," she said.

"Just take a deep breath, close your eyes, and picture the word in your head," Sam advised.

"You really think I can win?" Emily asked.

"You could," Sam said slowly. "If I wasn't still in the competition."

Sam smiled at his sister to show that he was teasing, but Emily wasn't so sure. Sam didn't like to lose at anything.

When the break was over, Mrs. Gunther started round four. Josh was up first.

"Your word is *whether*," Mrs. Gunther said.

"Can you use it in a sentence?" Josh asked.

"He couldn't decide whether or not he wanted to go," she said.

Josh smiled and correctly spelled the word.

Michelle was next. "Your word is *weather*," Mrs. Gunther said.

Michelle looked confused. "Didn't we just have that word?"

"No, this is a different word," Mrs. Gunther said. "I'll use it in a sentence for you. The weather in the summer is nicer than in the winter."

"Oh, I get it," Michelle said. "*Weather. W-e-a-t-h-e-r. Weather.*"

"That's correct," Mrs. Gunther said.

Emily was next. The pressure was on. Two people were already through to the next round.

"Emily, your word is *receipt*," Mrs. Gunther said.

Emily's face went white. It was one of those "*i* before e, except after *c*" words, but she couldn't remember whether or not the word *receipt* followed the rule. She stalled for time while she thought about it.

"Can you use the word in a sentence?" Emily asked.

"The owner gave her a receipt for the purchase," Mrs. Gunther said.

Emily's heart pounded in her chest. She wasn't sure of the order of the *i* and the *e*. She started to panic, but then remembered her brother's advice. She took a deep breath and closed her eyes. She tried to picture *receipt* on her list of spelling words.

Without opening her eyes, she said, "*Receipt. R-e-c-e-i-p-t. Receipt.*"

"Correct," said Mrs. Gunther. Emily finally opened her eyes.

"Okay, Sam," Mrs. Gunther said. "Your word is *beggar.*"

Sam frowned for a moment. Did the word end in *e-r* or *a-r*? He was pretty sure it was *a-r*, so that's what he went with. He was right! Drew clapped loudly as Sam advanced to the next round.

"Okay, Josh, we're back to you," Mrs. Gunther said. "Your word is *weird.*"

RECIEP
IE
RECEIPT
USE THIS
DING DING DING
IE

"*Weird. W-e-a-r-d. Weird,*" Josh said.

"I'm sorry, but that's incorrect," Mrs. Gunther said. "The correct spelling is *w-e-i-r-d.*"

Josh trudged back to his chair.

Michelle also stumbled, misspelling the word *continent.*

Emily was next and correctly spelled *science.* She remembered that it was another word that didn't follow the "*i* before *e,* except after *c*" rule.

Sam got the word *stomach* and spelled it with no problem.

"And then there were two," he said to Emily.

The Final Showdown

"Now that we're down to two spellers, I'll go back and forth between the two of you," Mrs. Gunther explained. "If both of you get it right, we'll keep going. The same thing will happen if both of you get it wrong. If only one of you spells their word correctly, that person will be the winner. Do you both understand?" Emily and Sam nodded.

For the next six rounds, both Emily and Sam spelled their words correctly.

Finally, in the twelfth round, Emily stumbled.

"*Vertical. V-e-r-t-i-c-l-e. Vertical,*" Emily said.

"I'm sorry, but that's incorrect," Mrs. Gunther said.

"It's *c-a-l,* isn't it?" Emily asked.

Mrs. Gunther nodded. "But you're not out yet. Sam has to spell his word correctly in order to win."

The teacher turned to Sam, who looked very confident. "Okay, Sam," Mrs. Gunther said. "Your word is *friend.*"

Sam smiled. It was an easy word. He was about to become the class spelling bee champion. Before he could begin to spell, however, Drew yelled "Go Sam!" from the back of the classroom. That's when Sam remembered what Drew had told him in the cafeteria. "You are my friend," Drew had said, and even spelled the word out for him. A smile came over Sam's face.

"Friend," he said, locking eyes with Drew. *"F-r-e-n-d. Friend."*

At the back of the room, Drew clapped his hands. "Good job, Sam!" he called out.

At the front of the room, Emily looked on in amazement while Mrs. Gunther shook her head and said, "I'm sorry, but that's incorrect."

Emily gave her brother a strange look. Mrs. Gunther referred to her list of words for the next round. "Emily, it's back to you. Your word is *dessert.*"

Emily paused for a moment. She knew there was a trick for remembering the difference between *desert* and *dessert,* but what was it? One word had one *s* and the other had two. Then it came to her: you always want extra dessert, so that was the one with the extra *s.*

"Dessert. D-e-s-s-e-r-t. Dessert," she spelled.

"Correct," Mrs. Gunther said. "Sam, your word is '*intentional*'."

Without even taking a breath, Sam spelled, *"Intentional. I-n-t-e-n-t-i-o-n-a-l. Intentional."*

"Correct," Mrs. Gunther said.

On and on they went, first Emily spelling her word correctly and then Sam.

Emily finally broke on the twenty-first round. Her word was *resistance.*

"Resistance. R-e-s-i-s-t-e-n-c-e. Resistance," she said.

"I'm sorry, but that's not correct," Mrs. Gunther said. "Sam, if you get this one right, you'll be the class spelling bee champion. Your word is *accommodate.*"

Sam looked up in surprise. Emily could tell that it was a new word for him. She didn't remember it being on the practice list of words. Sam had been confident in each round, but now he seemed unsure of himself. He shifted nervously from one foot to the other.

Sam looked over at Emily, who took a deep breath and closed her eyes. Sam smiled, understanding that his sister was giving him the same advice he had given her. He closed his eyes and took a deep breath.

He calmly said, *"Accommodate. A-c-c-o-m-m-o-d-a-t-e. Accommodate."*

"Congratulations, Sam," Mrs. Gunther said while the rest of the class applauded. But no one clapped louder than Emily and Drew.

Sam's Fable

The next morning, Emily knocked lightly on the door to Sam's bedroom.

"Yeah?" Sam called out.

"Do you want to go to the park with Mateo and me?" Emily asked.

"I'm busy," he answered.

"Busy doing what?"

"Homework."

"We don't have any homework," Emily said as she poked her head in the door.

"I do," Sam answered without looking up from his desk.

"We're in the same class," Emily said. "How can you have homework that I don't have?"

"Okay, okay," Sam said, giving in. "I'm working on our fable."

"But you won the class spelling bee," Emily said. "That means you won the bet and I have to write the fable, remember?"

"Yeah, but . . ."

"Yeah, but what?" Emily asked. "I thought you didn't like to read and write."

"Well, this whole literary unit turned out to be more interesting than I thought it would be," Sam admitted. "Anyway, I thought I could try writing our fable."

"Really?" Emily asked in amazement. "You're doing homework you don't have to do?"

"If it's no good, we can use yours instead," Sam said.

"Sounds like a deal," Emily replied.

When Emily returned home two hours later, she found Sam in his usual Saturday spot, munching chips in front of the television.

"Give up already?" Emily asked.

"Nope, I'm done," Sam replied.

"You finished it already?"

"Yep," Sam said. "Here, read it yourself."

He tossed his notebook to his sister. She sat on the couch and began to read.

The Prince Who Wanted to Become King

Once there was a prince who wanted to become king.

"Before you can become king, you must first prove yourself to be brave," the king told the prince.

"How can I do that?" the prince asked.

"A brave king will protect all the people in his kingdom," the king replied.

The prince went throughout the kingdom and found a small boy hiding in the shadow of the castle wall.

"Why are you hiding?" asked the prince.

"There is a new knight in the kingdom who is pushing everyone around," said the boy.

"You must show me where he is," said the prince.

"Um, he's right behind you," said the boy.

The prince turned around and there was the knight! His armor was shiny and golden, and he was holding a huge sword. The knight looked so spectacular in his armor that at first the prince couldn't believe he was bad.

"Out of my way!" the knight commanded. The knight's words did not match the sparkle of his armor and the prince could now see him for what he was.

"No, I will not let you pass," the prince said as he drew his own sword.

Seeing the prince's sword, the knight turned and ran away.

The prince went back to the king and told him what he had done.

"Can I be king now?" asked the prince.

"Before you can become king, you must first prove yourself to be kind," the king told the prince.

"How can I do that?" the prince asked.

"A kind king will take care of all the people in his kingdom," the king said.

The prince went throughout the kingdom and found many people in need of help. For a hungry family, he provided a cow and some chickens, so they would always have milk and eggs to eat. For a homeless family, he provided a house so they would always have a roof over their heads. For a sick man, he provided a doctor to help him get better.

The prince went back to the king and told him what he had done.

"Can I be king now?" asked the prince.

"Before you can become king, you must first prove yourself to be wise," the king told the prince.

"How can I do that?" the prince asked.

"That one you will have to figure out on your own," the king said.

The prince walked away. He didn't know how he could show the king he was wise. So, he turned to the person he always went to for advice: his sister.

"Princess, in order for me to become king, I must first prove that I am wise," the prince said.

"You just did," answered the princess. "By asking someone else when you don't know the answer, you have proven yourself wise."

The prince thought about this for a long time. Finally, he went back to the king.

"Your highness," said the prince. "I have decided that my sister and I should rule together."

The king smiled. "You have indeed proven yourself wise, my son. From this day forward, the kingdom shall be ruled by the two of you."

And that's just what they did.

Emily looked up from the notebook.

"Well, what do you think?" asked Sam anxiously.

"It's alright," Emily said.

"Alright?" Sam asked. "Just alright?" He looked crushed.

"Okay, it's really good," Emily admitted. "I just didn't want you to get a big head. I mean, you already won the class spelling bee."

"Just barely," Sam said. "You almost pulled off a tortoise and the hare thing. How'd you learn to spell all of those words so quickly?"

"It's called studying," Emily replied. "And it sounds like you actually paid attention to some of those fables. I thought you didn't like reading and writing."

"Well, they weren't as bad as I thought they were going to be," Sam said.

"I told you so," Emily said.

"Yeah, well don't tell anybody I might actually like reading and writing," Sam replied. "I have a reputation, you know."

"It's our little secret," Emily said. "But I can't wait to tell them that you can't rule a kingdom without me."

Sam grabbed a couch cushion, but Emily ran out of the living room before he could throw it at her.

Sam smiled. "I guess running a kingdom with Emily wouldn't be the worst thing," he said.

The End

Let's Learn Some More!

Who was Aesop?

Aesop was a storyteller who lived in Greece more than 2,500 years ago. Not much is known about his life, but historians believe he was an enslaved person who won his freedom. After that, he traveled around the Greek empire and told stories. He became famous for his fables. A fable is a special kind of story that teaches a lesson. Aesop's fables have been told over and over for thousands of years.

One of Aesop's most famous fables is called *The Boy Who Cried Wolf*. The story is about a shepherd boy who wanted some company. He ran into the valley yelling "Wolf! Wolf!" to get people's attention. The farmers in the area ran out to meet him. Of course, they didn't find a wolf, but they stayed and talked with the boy for a while. A few days later, the boy tried the same trick again. He cried "Wolf! Wolf!" and the farmers came running. Again, no wolf, but they stayed and kept the boy company for a while. A few days later, a real wolf came out of the forest and began to steal the sheep. The boy yelled "Wolf! Wolf!" but this time the farmers didn't believe him. No one came to help him, and the wolf had a very good meal.

The moral of the story is that if you lie often, soon people won't believe anything you say.

A moral is like a lesson or a message about good behavior and bad behavior. Aesop knew that people don't like to be told when they do bad things. By telling stories with morals, Aesop was able to entertain people and point out how they should act at the same time.

Want to write your own fable?

It's easy to write your own fable. Just follow these steps:

1. Start with your moral: What lesson do you want readers to learn?
2. Pick your character: You can use an animal, person, plant, or object as your main character.
3. Pick your character's traits: Does your character have bad traits like being selfish, greedy, or mean? Or do they have good traits like being strong, wise, or hardworking?
4. Figure out the conflict: What problems or tricky situations does your character get into?

Write your fable: Remember that fables are usually short and simple, without a lot of details.

Acknowledgments

Thanks to the great team at Common Deer Press: Kirsten Marion for leading the team and helping to make this series happen, Erin Della Mattia and Emily Stewart for all the great ideas and superb editing, the marketing team, and everyone else working behind the scenes. Your work does not go unnoticed by me.

Thanks so much to Mattie Mitchell for the wonderful illustrations. I thought the pictures for the first two Emily and Sam books were amazing, and these top both of those!

Thanks to my family—Stephanie, Jordan, Justin, and Debbie—for everything . . . always.

A special thanks to all the readers of the Emily and Sam and The Math Kids series. I always love to hear from you. If you want to contact me or keep up with what's going on with Emily and Sam and the Math Kids, you can do so at their website at TheMathKids.com.

About the Author

Dave Cole has degrees in math and computer science and has shared his passion for education at many levels, including teaching at the college level, coaching elementary math teams, and running a summer math camp. He also has a love of writing and has written a number of plays as well as The Math Kids series (as David Cole). Find him at www.themathkids.com.

About the Illustrator

Matty Mitchel was born and raised in Australia but found his way to Seattle eleven years ago and has recently moved back to Fremantle, Western Australia with his wife, son, daughter, and dog. If Matty's not chasing (or being chased by) his two munchkins, he's drawing, and if he's not drawing, then he can be found making something creative, and if he's not creating something, then he is skateboarding, and if that's not the case, then he is probably snuggling with his lovely wife on the couch watching TV.